D0680453

And Off You Go to
Change the World

By Ashten Evans   Illustrated by Sabdo Purnomo

Published in the U.S. by:
ULYSSES PRESS
P. O. Box 3440
Berkeley, CA 94703
www.ulyssespress.com

ISBN: 978-1-64604-032-2
Library of Congress Control Number: 2020931851

Printed in Korea by Artin Printing Company through Four Colour Print Group
10 9 8 7 6 5 4 3 2 1

Acquisitions editor: Casie Vogel
Managing editor: Claire Chun
Editor: Julie Holland
Proofreader: Renee Rutledge
Cover design: Jake Flaherty
Illustrations: Sabdo Purnomo

One...

Two...

Three...

Four!

This is the day you've been waiting for!

A New Chapter Begins

You did it! You made it!
You are strong and smart.

You worked and learned
and made a great start.

Today is a big day—
a celebration, too.

Here are some wishes
I have for you...

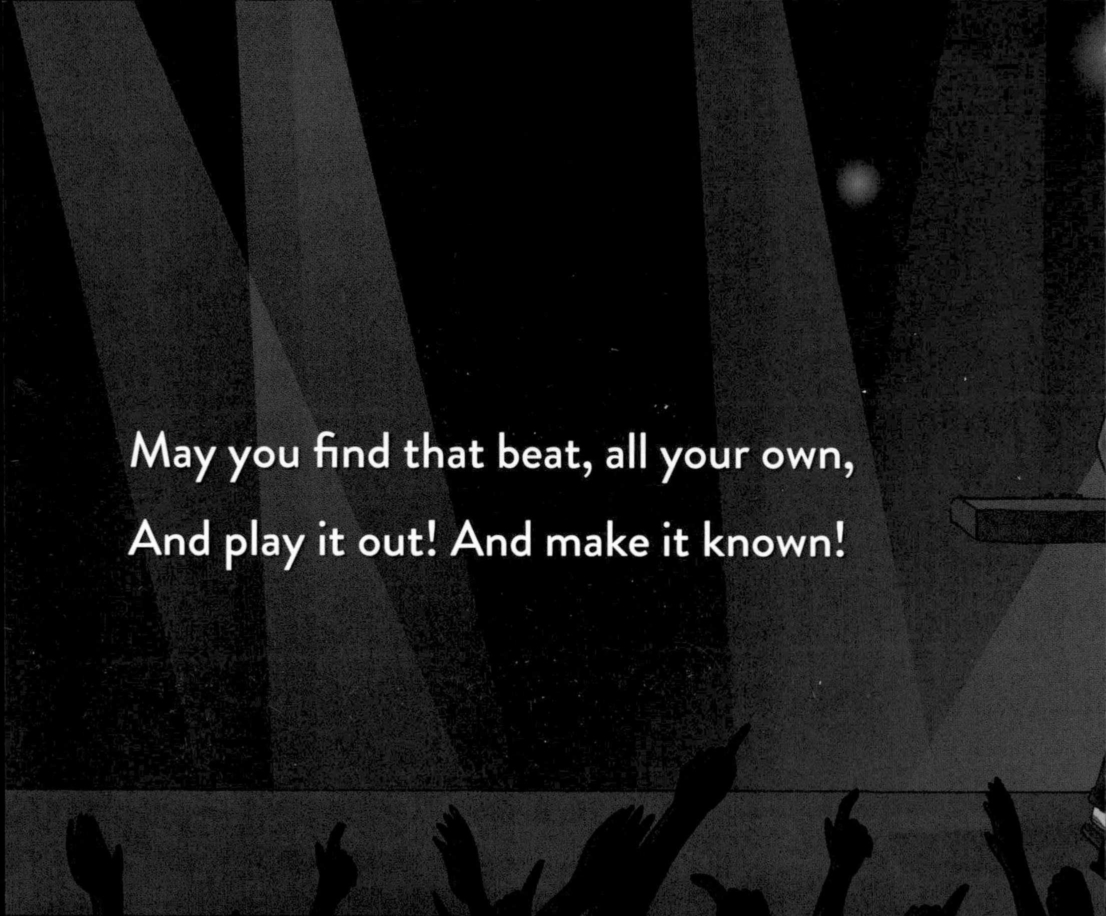

May you find that beat, all your own,
And play it out! And make it known!

And go as high
as the planets in space.

You will swoop and soar
from this starting place.

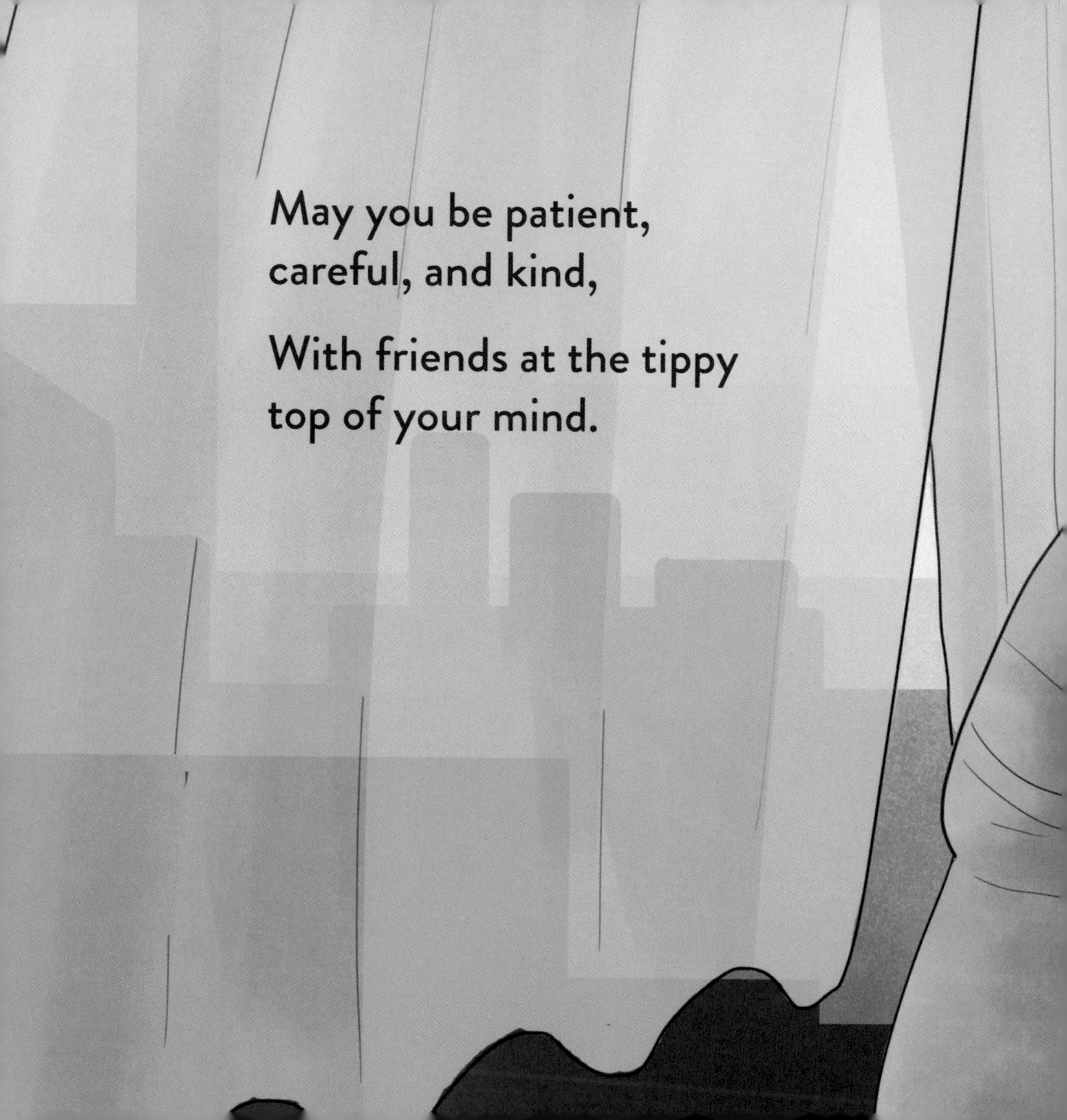

May you be patient,
careful, and kind,

With friends at the tippy
top of your mind.

And as those friendships
grow happy and true.

You will help others,
and they will help you.

May you stay curious and bold.
With a wee bit of zeal,

There will be no end
to the wonders you reveal.

And as your inventions
take to the sky,

Through ups and through downs,
never doubt you can fly.

May you have courage
when rising to fame

And the entire crowd
is shouting your name!

Or painting in colors,
dazzling and bright,

And bringing new creations
into the light.

May you share stories
of adventure and action,

Accepting praise
with humble satisfaction.

And share your joy with each song that you sing

Whether your melodies tremble or ring.

SING

May you be creative
when the world expects

That the problems you're facing
are too complex.

And solve tough puzzles
with new tools you find.

And stretch to the limits
the strengths of your mind.

STAR LAB
MILK

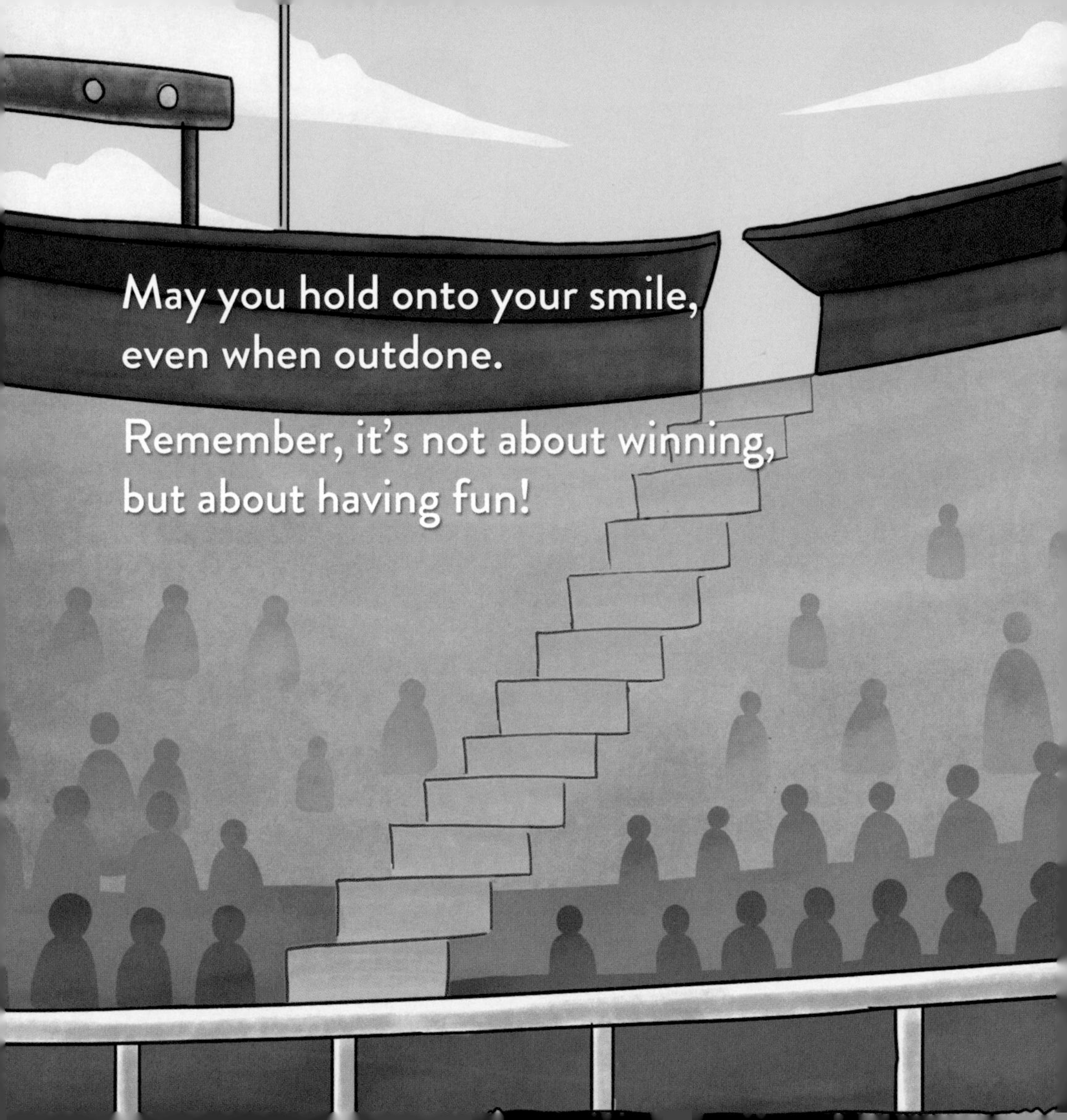

May you hold onto your smile,
even when outdone.

Remember, it's not about winning,
but about having fun!

7

And play for the joy
of each marvelous sport

Savoring each triumph,
whether long or short.

May you always explore
this mysterious place.

There is so much to find
on Earth and in space.

You might study life
in the deepest of seas

And discover new animals
by twos and by threes.

May all of your learnings
be seeds to be sown.

And inspire you to care
for our Earth that is home.

And to fight for what
you think is just,

Speaking up for what's right
when what's right is a must.

May you share what you craft—
whether fiction or fact.

What you give to the world
has amazing impact.

And listen to others,
and try to be fair,

Doing your best
to show that you care.

May your ideas become
hotter than hot

More needed and known
than ever you thought.

And your magnificent dreams
stand solid and steady,

So you can build on them
whenever you're ready.

May you stay inquisitive
and always explore.

Life holds many wonders
too great to ignore.

For you will keep learning
after school days are through.

You will find so many things
that interest you!

So go learn! Go grow!
Before you, life will unfurl.

And off you go
to change the world!

SCHOOL

Hooray

for You!

About the Author

Ashten Evans is an editor and writer living in New York City. She enjoys spending time with her loving husband, Drew, and their super chill cat, Chelsea. This is her first book.

About the Illustrator

Sabdo Purnomo is a professional children's book illustrator. He lives in Indonesia.